How Will I Get to School This Year?

Jerry Pallotta

SCHOLASTIC INC.

New York   Toronto   London   Auckland
Sydney   Mexico City   New Delhi   Hong Kong

David Biedrzycki

To Lucia Fraser, Maura White, and Katie McEachern,
three great teachers!

— J.P.

To Mr. Paul Brennan and my friends at
Riverside Elementary West, Taylor, PA,
my hometown. How will you get to school this year?

— D.B.

ISBN 978-0-545-26659-8

Text copyright © 2011 by Jerry Pallotta
Illustrations copyright © 2011 by David Biedrzycki

All rights reserved. Published by Scholastic Inc.
SCHOLASTIC and associated logos are trademarks
and/or registered trademarks of Scholastic Inc.

12 11 10 9 8 7 6 5 4 3 2 1   11 12 13 14 15 16/0

Printed in Singapore   46
First printing, September 2011

WELCOME BACK
STUDENTS
SCHOOL STARTS
WEDNESDAY WE
ARE LOOKING
FORWARD TO A
GREAT SCHOOL
YEAR

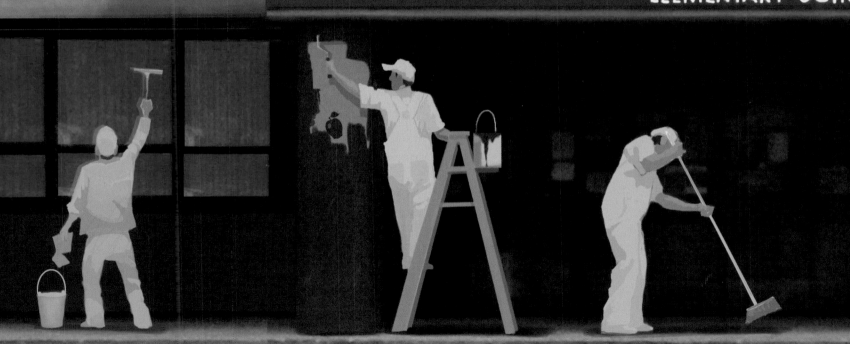

School starts tomorrow.

Last year, I got tired of taking the smelly school bus.

What if I went to school a different way?

I'll ride on a giant mosquito.

What will my classmates think?

A pig will provide a good ride.

I'll hog the highway.

Maybe flying on a bald eagle is faster.

Meet me at the flagpole!

I'll swing to school on a gorilla.

I don't mind banana breath.

Yippee! I could float to school.

A zillion butterflies will flap their wings for me.

Today's Lesson
Spelling Words

coral
clam
claw
crab

I'll swim to class on a hammerhead.

But where will I park the shark?

Who needs a bus?

I'll be riding a giant tarantula.

I can walk to school. No bullies will bother me.

I'll be protected by a pride of lionesses.

I can sit back and relax.

It's sweet to be delivered by two grizzlies.

I could hop to school with a family of frogs.

Did they forget their backpacks?

I could commute in the mouth of a white tiger.

Uh-oh! She thinks she's my mother.

Could a tortoise get me to school on time?

I wouldn't want to miss lunch.

There are many ways to get to school.
But it's more fun when I go with my friends.

The school bus is here!

I love school. I can't wait to go back.